I0530736

A MILLION PIECES

THE BECOMING UNBROKEN TRILOGY

by Analuisa Flores

3Dog ArtPress
Corona del Mar, CA

Copyright 2015 by Analuisa Flores

All rights reserved. This is a work of fiction. No part of this publication may be reproduced, stored in a retrieval system, or transmitted, in any form or by any means, electronic, mechanical, photocopying, recording, or otherwise, without the written prior permission of the author.

Published in the United States by 3DogArtPress, a division of 3DogArt.

ISBN: 978-0989638531

Edit and Format by Joanne Milo and Christy Jones
www.3DogArtPress.com

Cover Format by Ryan McCoy
www.Facebook.com/Fewtr.Technology

Cover Art by Denny Stoekenbroek
© "Dirrrty" original charcoal drawing, reprinted with permission from the artist, Danny Stoekenbroek.
http://www.dennystoekenbroek.com
"My name is Denny Stoekenbroek and I make drawings. Mostly with charcoal. I am a self-taught artist living in the south of The Netherlands. People are mostly the subject in my work. Sometimes it's soft and sometimes it's raw. But it's always with passion!"

I dedicate this book to the life that could
have ended a long while ago, but didn't.
Never end a story in the middle.

.
,

Acknowledgements

Words cannot describe how much I appreciate all the people who made this book happen. These are the people who encouraged me, and the people who helped publish it. Joanne and Richard Milo were probably the biggest help. They took me in and encouraged me to pursue my dreams. Without them, this book could not have been possible. So many more people helped along the way: my editors, Christy Jones, Monica Warthen and Joanne Milo; Ryan McCoy who helped with the cover art; Denny Stoekenbroek who created the beautiful artwork I used on the cover

My family was there for me when I was at my lowest, and without their help, I wouldn't have been able to write from the heart. My sister, Luisana Lopez, always encouraged me to write and my mother, Felicitas, was there for me, even from a distance, and never let me fall through the cracks. I love you all for what you have helped me accomplish and I love you all for being the kindest souls I will ever meet.

And there are so many who encouraged me and loved me through my journey: Jonathan Brian Elias Macedo, Marissa Mojica, Calli Joy Morrow, Brenda Chavero, Christian Gallardo, Randi Dentt, Mrs. Sixtos (Remington elementary school) and Mrs. Roseth (early college high school). I thank you ALL from the bottom of my heart!

Chapter 1

"Though my soul may set in darkness,
it will rise in perfect light;
I have loved the stars too fondly
to be fearful of the night."
~ Sarah Williams

Logan

I step out into the vast darkness. The skies circle above me in a never-ending black hole. Swirls of black and silvers line the sky and I can't help but admire the ironic beauty of it all. I close my eyes for a moment and try to picture what the world looked like before the darkness fell upon it. I can imagine the blue skies and the sun's warmth beating down on my face. I can remember my parents tucking my sister and me into bed and telling us stories of what it was like before; but of course, those are just old folk tales passed down generations of ancestors.

I lose myself and can almost feel the warmth creeping over me from head to toe. I lost hope in ever seeing my child-like fantasies becoming a reality when they left. The moment ends and I'm brought back to my desolate reality. I can hear Emily's wheezing, coming through her open window. I go back in the house to close it. She opens it every night, despite my tactics, in hopes that the sun will rise and she'll awake to a better day. I know better than to hope for what will never come. I close the window and head out once again. I see the dim light of the street lanterns turn off since the day has officially begun.

Paityn

Red-hot tears fall; they stain the pearl white bathroom floor. They're filled with grief and fear. The grief comes from the fact that her parents left, once and for all. And the fear comes from the fact I was doing it again. Blade in hand, I remember how hard it was to stop the last time. They stopped me. Who will stop me this time? I'd like to call them a necessary evil, in a way. They made me stop and take a good look in the mirror when I lost control, like now.

But they got in the way, they always got in the way; I'm glad they're gone. I'm glad I'm alone, no more baggage, nothing left to lose.

I hear pounding on the door. It's here. Faster than last time, oh how I've missed this. Sweet death will never be mine to take and I'm angry about it. Anger is a very ugly emotion but at least I have emotions. They don't, they do what they're programmed to do. They've busted through the front door. Tick Tock. Come and find me, Robo-Freak. I still have a good 30 seconds before I black out. Tick Tock. I'm woozy. Focus, Paityn, turn around and face it.

5

I see it; it's as beautiful as I remember. Darkness falls and the game begins once again.

Logan

For our type of people, we only have two choices of jobs. We can either build them or we can fix them. I'm too young and have very little education to fix them, so I build them. I've never seen them completed since I work at the beginning stage of the process. I attach two red wires to the motherboard and connect them with a green. Nothing I need an education for. Each stage has its own warehouse, there are about twenty warehouses chained together to build them. Each day I do the same thing over and over; some people have gone mad doing it.

The only thing that keeps me sane is my sister. She needs me and I can't let her down. 3 hours done, 8 more to go.

Red *click* Red *click* Green *click* Repeat.

I bet they're beautiful. I can just imagine it, the pristine glass outer shell and the strong unbreakable inner computer.

Red *click* Red *click* Green *click*.

I want to see it just once, just so I know what I'm building. I can sneak into warehouse 20 ... What am I thinking? I'm going mad, I think. I can't risk that; Emily needs me.

Red *click* Red *click* Green *click*.

I can try to ... kill myself. I mean I wouldn't really kill myself, but if I tried to, they would come for me and rehabilitate me. They would just bring me back home after they saw it was an accident.

My thoughts were suddenly stopped by the loud wailing noise coming from the speakers. We only have them for morning announcements, other than that I had never heard anything come from the speakers. The younger people seemed confused and were looking around to see what was happening while covering their ears.

"There must have been a suicide attempt," murmured an older man to his neighbor.

"You think? I mean, what man would be dumb enough to do that?" the neighbor rebutted.

8

"Maybe he was just curious, and wanted to see the Safety-Robos?" I piped in.

They both gawked at me as if I had said something incredibly stupid. I felt myself turn red in embarrassment. I started to turn away when the older man placed his hand on my shoulder.

"Sonny, no one wants to see those things. Dontcha know what's really goin' on here?" he asked.

"What do you mean?" I asked inquisitively.

"If you're taken away by those things, you're never comin' back." His eyes had gone all wide and crazy looking.

"That's not true, they heal you, then bring you back to your old life," I argued.

"Sonny, you have no idea what kinda world you be livin' in," and with that, he turned away and went back to his conversation with his neighbor.

That can't be true. It just can't be. He's a crazy old man. The Safety-Robos are built to help us, not take us away forever.

9

Mr. Krebs comes in with a loud bang. He walks calmly to the speaker and uses a remote to turn it off. He starts speaking into his remote but his voice booms out of the speakers.

"Warehouse 1, as you already know, there has been a breech in warehouse 20. Because of this, we ask you to not panic and to go home for the day. I'm sorry to say, it will be without pay. We understand that this is a huge inconvenience and we do apologize. All of you should take something away from this little mishap. Life will always be worth living. I hope you have a good rest of your day, and we will see you all tomorrow. Thank you."

Everyone starts walking out in a herd. I linger behind, out of pure curiosity. I hide under my station and I overhear Mr. Krebs talking to one of the guards.

"Is the situation under control?" Mr. Krebs asks in a more serious tone.

"Yes Sir, the young lady has been captured and is under our surveillance as we speak," the guard responded in the same serious tone.

"A young lady? I thought some stupid worker tried to kill himself again."

"No Sir, a young lady crashed Warehouse 20's whole shipment for the next 2 months."

"What! Why does no one tell me anything! Imbeciles!"

I hear him stalk away, the guard soon after.

Paityn

Left. I can hear them. All I see are endless hallways. All I hear is my heart pounding. Right. Don't get caught. I keep running, never stop running,

I've studied the layout of this building a million times; I know it has to be around here somewhere. Right. They're getting closer. If they get me, it's over. It can't end this way. I need more time. I stop at a fork. No, this can't be right; there was no fork in the layout.

I can't go back, they can't be far behind. I can hear them, 7 of them. Think Paityn, think. I look around frantically. I look up and see the furnace.

Logan

I follow them. I don't know why my feet take control. The building has so many hallways, with twists and turns, so I follow their voices. I hear a group of guards running towards me so I rush into a nearby utility closet. About twenty guards run past the closet and once they're gone, I'm lost. I can't hear Mr. Krebbs anymore. Damn it. What now? My better judgment takes over and I make my way back into the main building station. It feels so weird being alone here. It seems bigger now that it's just me.

CRASH #*@ BANG @#* CLANG!

I'm slammed to the ground by something. Face down, I try to lift myself up but my left arm doesn't respond. I use my right; once I stand, all I see is rubble all around me.

"Where is she?!?" someone yells behind me.

"Don't move!" another yells.

I turn slowly, still clutching my left arm.

"I'm a worker here, something fell on me and I'm hurt." I say calmly.

They all look at me with confused looks. Then they start mumbling to each other.

"He doesn't know, does he?"

"Maybe he's with HER."

"No, you can't fake a broken arm."

A guard walks toward me.

"Kid, what happened here?" one of the guards asks.

"Something fell from the ceiling," I responded.

He turns to the rest of the group and nods.

"Guys, he's ok. Take him to M.H 12."

I cut him off. "M.H 12?!? What's that?" I ask frantically.

They all chuckle.

"Don't worry kid. M.H 12 is where they patch up non self-inflicted injuries."

I let a sigh of relief. I didn't want to never come back; like that old man had warned me about. Out of curiosity, I ask,

"Do you know what fell on me? It felt heavier than a ceiling tile."

"Kid, it wasn't a "what" that fell on you; it was a "who," he responded. That girl the guards said destroyed a month's worth of shipment.

Chapter 2

"Learning to let go should be learned
before learning to get.
Life should be touched, not strangled.
You've got to relax, let it happen at times, and
at others move forward with it."
~ Ray Bradbury

Logan

By the time I got home, Emily was ready to just about kill me. I sit down in the kitchen.

"Where were you!?" she yells the second I walked through the door.

"Em. I was at work."

"Don't you Em me, you liar, James said you all got to leave hours ago!"

"James?" I look up at her with curiosity.

"Yea. James. He works with you. Just started actually. Don't change the subject!"

I tell her the whole story. I don't keep things from her, ever since our parents went away. After all that, we had dinner and went to bed, like every workday. I stay up thinking about what happened at the factory. A girl. One girl took down a two-month shipment. How does something like that happen? I stayed up thinking about her and, at one point or another; I fell asleep.

I woke up at the break of dawn, again. Went through my morning routine and went to work. When I got there, I was surprised to see all the workers outside, and the factory doors locked. Again I saw Mr. Krebbs. I got there just in time for him to tell us the factory will be closed for another two weeks. A lot of people were angry and upset. Me, not so much.

I walked home and decided to pick up something for Emily. As kids, our parents saved every penny, so we never really received gifts or sweets. But once a year, on our birthday, we would get a choice: a sweet or a birthday meal. It was always the sweet (our mother wasn't the best cook). I had to take a trip to the Emerald City; only my sister and I call it that, since our parents forced us to watch an ancient film from their great-great grandparents' childhood.

Two hover-shuttles and a thirty-minute walk later, I was in the city. I could see all the glimmering, metallic-colored buildings; connected interways overhead with beautiful people driving around in lavish hover-cars. I took all the beauty in and let myself imagine, for just a moment that this was my life. Then I shook off that fantasy and walked on. Interways were ideal to move around in the city but some of the shops had set up down below to attract outer city people. Nothing as extravagant as the up-above shops but nice enough to make the trip worthwhile. I had only been there once before, to buy Emily a gift for her first birthday after the incident. I wasn't completely sure the sweet shop would still be there but it was worth a shot.

Sure enough it was. I walked into a quaint shop, wall-to-wall full of sweets and treats. I was the only one there, so it seemed. I didn't know where to start looking so I headed to the front counter to find someone who could help.

An hour later, and half a bag full of sweets, I walked out of the shop feeling swindled. Everything sounded so good, and I think Emily deserves the best. I walked out and the "sun" is out and everyone in the city is having another amazing day. One day, I'll be able to live here with Emily. She'll go to real classes to be a real nurse. She should get anything she wants, but we don't live in that kind of reality. I'll work my whole life just to get by, Emily will keep going to our neighbor's house and learn to kind-of be a nurse, and at eighteen, I'll marry her off like I'm supposed to. She'll be a wonderful wife and have beautiful children. I want so much more for her.

I look up at the complex interweb of what could be called highways and streets. From down here, it looks like a spider web. All the streets and highways lead to a center building, which is known as the Crown Building.

Not only is it called that because it looks like a shimmering jewel incrusted crown, but that's where the hierarchy meets to "protect the interests of the common person," which so happens to be engraved above the entranceway. I chuckle at the thought. More than half of the population lives in the slums, working in factories for minimum wage, if that, to barely get by. But the rest of the population, those born into that life, or are related to or are friends with the hierarchy, they get the good life. They are all connected, like the spider web that makes up their city.

I'm about to turn back to catch the hover-shuttle home when I hear the city alert system blare behind me. I look up and see a picture of the most beautiful thing I've seen in my short life. Piercing black eyes with matching wavy hair. Her picture flashes for a good minute or two. Then a video message from the Hierarchy comes one.

"Attention. Attention. We are looking for this deviant. Anyone with information about her or her whereabouts, please inform your local authorities. She is a high risk to the public and needs to be caught. Thank you for your time and enjoy the rest of your day."

I walk on. How could someone so beautiful be a high risk?

Paityn

Perfect. The whole fucking city has seen my face. I walk in the shadows. Not that it's likely anyone would notice. They are all in their own world. Imbeciles. All of them. In their own perfect world. HA!

My stomach growls. If I get under the city, I might be able to show my face. I take an old, broken, sewage tube since the only way out of the city is by hover-cars. Good thing I'm not claustrophobic. Damn it, it stinks in here. I'm out. Down here, rules don't apply. People steal from each other, lie, and only look out for themselves.

I stay in the shadows because there is probably a reward out for me. I see a boy walking with a bag of candy. It looks delicious. I can take him. He turns in my direction as if he can read my mind. He's beautiful. My eyes devour his every feature. Tan skin. Strong build. Confident stance. Dark brown hair. And those eyes. Emerald green. So piercing, they almost invite you into the soul. Most people have soul-less eyes, but he doesn't. He's beautiful, in every sense of the word.

Paityn! Snap out of it! I can't do it. I could do it to a person who doesn't actually have a soul, but he's the only one around. This is life and death. You have to survive. You can't end it here, ok? He's mine.

I walk in step with him, hidden in the shadows. He turns toward me again, as if he can feel my presence. He quickens his pace. I need to strike before he gets away. I get close enough to shove him in an alley without him seeing me. I hide behind some garbage bags. He regains his balance and frantically looks around. He's bigger than me, so I need to use his weight against him. I pounce out and end up on top of him.

Knock him out and walk away, Paityn. You only want the candy. I slam his head on the ground. He reaches for my arms. We roll around: punching, kicking, on top, on the bottom. He gets the upper hand and his whole body on top of me, pinning me to the ground.

"Who are you!" he yells.

I spit in his face. He wipes it off but he's too strong and I can't get away.

"Are you going to explain?" he asks, in a more gentle tone.

"The stupid candy," I reply weakly.

"That's all you wanted?" he asked.

I weakly nod.

"Why didn't you just ask? I'd be glad to share, I bought too much anyway."

He gets off of me and walks over to the bag of candy that had flown to the other end of the alley. I sit there pleasantly surprised when he walks back over and opens the bag to me.

"Here, have some. My sister and I don't need all this anyway," he reassures me. Who is this guy?

"Thank you."
I grab a handful and stash some in my pocket and then eat a piece. He's staring at me. Shit. He recognizes me. I look up into his beautiful emerald eyes and he returns the favor.

"It's you," he says.
I turn and run.

Logan

I grab her. What am I doing?

"Don't run. I won't hurt you."

"How do I know to trust you?!?" she frantically responds.

"Because you attacked me and I still helped you?" I responded.

Crap. Just let her go, Logan. She stares at me with those deep black eyes.

"Okay. I won't go. Will you let me go now?" She slightly cocks her head to one side. That. Was. Adorable.

"Okay."

I let go and she doesn't run. She just stares at me.

"I'm Logan," I stick my hand out. Smooth Logan. Real smooth.

She steps back, and then looks from my hand back up to me.

"I'm Paityn."

"I know," I point up to the city where her picture is still up, she blushes embarrassingly and looks at her feet.

"Don't worry. I won't turn you in." I reassure her.

"Why?" She seems so puzzled.

"I don't know."

"I need to go," she says, still staring at me.

"Where?"

"I don't know."

"I could help you. You can stay at my house." Where the hell did that come from?

"Why are you helping me? Don't you see I'm a "high risk" person! Are you insane?!?"

"No. I'm not. I was raised to question everything. Just because a sign says you're bad doesn't mean you are."

She looked dumbfounded, like she couldn't comprehend my compassion.

"Ok."

And we walked, simple as that. We couldn't risk using public transit so we walked in silence. What am I getting myself into?

Paityn

What am I doing? He could be leading me to my death ... I don't think he is, though. We walk for what seemed forever. Night falls and it makes me a little more at ease. It's harder to recognize me in the dark. Logan looks a little tense.

"Are you ok?" I ask calmly.

"No. Emily's probably freaking out," he says plainly.

Emily? Girlfriend maybe? Of course he has a girlfriend. Wait, why do I care?

"Will she be ok with another girl in the house?" I ask, trying to keep my cool.

"Emily? Oh yea. She's always wanted a sister. Always tells me I should have been a girl."

"Emily's your sister?!?" Did my voice just crack? God no.

"Of course, why would you think otherwise?" He replies coolly.

"Well, you look of age and so I just assumed." Why am I so relieved?

"No. I take care of my sister, no time to find a girl worthwhile."

He's so straightforward. Maybe it's me that's making him tense. We keep walking. Once we get closer to a residence area, Logan hands me his jacket.

"Here, it's cold. And people like to sit outside at night," he says nonchalant.

"Thanks, for everything," I reply simply because I can't think of anything that would measure up to exactly how much I appreciate he's done thus far.

We stop in front of a little house, really a shack. All the windows are open, which surprises me. Is it safe here? How could a girl home alone leave all the windows open? Logan opens the door and walks in first. I guess Mr. Perfect isn't as chivalrous as I thought. We are bombarded with a screaming girl.

"Where were you?!? James told me you didn't have work today. I sat here worried sick!"
Maybe he walked in first to protect me.

"Em. Calm down, we have a guest."
He steps out of the way and she looks at me, hard. Does she recognize me? I'm doomed.

"Hi, I'm Paityn."

"Oh. I'm so sorry. You must think I'm so rude."
She walks over to me and wraps her arms around me.
Why is she touching me?

"I'm Emily, Logan calls me Em," she continues.

"Nice to meet you." Oh this is so awkward.
We all look at each other for what feels like minutes.

"She's staying with us for a while," Logan says
to break the silence.

"Oh my god. I finally get a sister?!?"
Sister? Who is this chick! Is she for real?
Logan nudges at Emily.

"Em, I think you're scaring her." He chuckles
to himself.
Me. Scared, nah? More like terrified.

"I'm still upset at you. Just because we have a
guest doesn't mean you can come home this late,"
Emily huffs.

"I brought you candy?"
He shakes the bag in front of her and smirks. She looks
at the bag like a piece of gold. She jumps up and hugs
Logan. Her shirt raises enough to see the side of her
stomach. Are those scars? No! They can't be! No way!
Could she be the girl they're looking for?

31

We have dinner, which tastes amazing; probably because it's my first meal in weeks. I'm mostly observing Logan and Emily at dinner. They seem so happy to have each other, now that Emily's anger has subsided. They laugh and talk, and I find it so fascinating. So light does exist in this never-ending black hole. Damn it, did she just ask me a question?

"I'm sorry, what did you say?" I question. They both giggle at me.

"What?" I respond.

"Emily just asked you if you wanted more food," Logan motions towards Emily.

"I can have more?" I say, with a little too much excitement in my voice. They giggle again. Who are these people? How the heck do they have so much food to spare?

"Of course! You can have as much as you want," she says with giggles under her breath.

"Thank you, I'm okay for now," I reply, thinking of nothing else to say.

"So when am I meeting this mysterious James that keeps ratting me out?" Logan says to Emily.

"You work with him, introduce yourself, maybe we can have him over for dinner."

"I'd rather not, we already have one guest to take care of."

Logan looks up from his plate and winks at me. What was that? It was kind of cute.

"No fair! You brought a girl home. Why can't I bring a boy?"

Logan's face drops and his tone gets serious.

"Em, the difference is Paityn has nowhere else to go. I'll think about James coming to dinner, ok?"

With that, Emily gets quiet. She looks me directly in the eyes as she apologizes.

"I'm sorry, I didn't mean it that way, Paityn. Thank you, Logan."

I like her ...

"Oh you're fine. No offense taken."

Half an hour later, Logan is setting up his bed with clean sheets for me. After fighting about it for 15 minutes, I gave up. He said he would sleep on the floor. I stand back and just watch him. He's so graceful, yet so rugged. When he finishes, he catches me staring.

"Like what you see?"

I blush involuntarily.

"What do you mean?" I reply.

"The bed," he says with that smile that makes my knees weak.

"Oh yes! Sorry. For putting you out, I mean."

"It's all right, it's nice to have company. I would have given you the whole room but Emily is very touchy about her privacy."

"I understand." More than you know, actually.

Logan tells me he has to close up the house and then he would come back. He left, leaving me to my own devices. I walk out of Logan's bedroom and knock on Emily's door. I hear some shuffling and banging before she opens the door, looking winded.

"Hey Paityn, what's up?" she says, almost out of breathe.

"Oh, was I interrupting something? I can come back later." God Paityn, can you make the situation any more awkward?

"Oh it's fine, come in."
She really needs to stop the whole Stepford Wife bit.

I walk into her room, not surprised in the slightest. Pristine white bedding with pillows to match. Everything has a place and is in its place; I see nothing

34

out of the ordinary. Wow I'm impressed, even I couldn't hide it this well.

"Your room is beautiful."

"Thank you." she says plainly.

Fuck, Paityn. Just get to the point.

"Can we talk?"

"Sure. What did you want to talk about?"

Logan walks in and sees me. He seems so surprised to see me in the same room with Emily.

"Oh, I didn't think you were in here. I was just going to say goodnight to Em."

Upon hearing her name, Emily responds almost automatically.

"Goodnight Logan, thank you for the candy. It was very kind of you."

I take my out quite urgently.

"I guess I'll head off with Logan. We can talk later."

"You don't have to leave. Logan won't mind, right Logan?"

She seemed so disappointed that I was about to leave. I can't ask her about her scars with Logan around. He would flip.

"Not at all, you can stay if you'd like, don't leave on my account."

Maybe she wants to talk about it just as much I want to listen.

"I'm kind of tired. We can talk tomorrow Em, promise. I'm not going anywhere."

With that she seems reassured that we would talk soon. We say our goodnights, and Logan and I walk out of Em's room.

Logan

Ok Logan, be cool.

She walks in ahead of me and I can't help but stare. She's graceful but I know from experience that she's powerful. She turns and catches me staring; I look away. Smooth move, Casanova.

"Um, well, this is awkward. I've never had a girl alone in my room before." I say, thinking of nothing else to say.

I see her go wide eyed and blush. Why did I just say that out loud? Dammit Logan, can you be anymore lame?

"I didn't mean it like that."

"Oh it's ok. I know what you meant. Thank you for being so kind towards me. It's quite refreshing."

"What do you mean?"

"I mean that I've never met someone like you; someone willing to help a complete stranger. It's a new concept to me. All I've known is rejection and malice when it comes to people, even before I was turned into a "high risk" person."

"Well I guess you've been hanging around the wrong kind of people." I smirk.

She blushes. Wow, for a complete badass that can kick my ass, she sure does blush a lot.

With that, we say our goodnights and she slips under my sheets. Why do I find that so attractive? I lay down on the little nest I made for myself using our extra blankets and pillows. I had to whack out all the dust since we haven't had any guests in a long time. I stay up thinking about Paityn. This is the girl that brought down a two-month shipment of highly integrated technology. I have to learn more about her. After an hour or two, I fall asleep.

Chapter 3

"You've got to live,
no matter how many skies have fallen."
~ D.H Lawrence

Logan

Purely out of habit, I wake up before sunrise. I get up as quietly as I can and am surprised to see that Paityn isn't in my bed. Where the hell did she go? Em! I shoot up off the floor and run into Em's room. She is sound asleep, and doesn't even stir with all the commotion I just made. I walk into the living area and there is no sign of Paityn anywhere. Maybe she left. That would be a whole lot easier for me. But why do I feel so disappointed? I hear the floor creak. I whip around ready to attack and see Paityn standing behind me with a cup of water. She steps back, just as startled as I am.

"Sorry did I scare you?"

"No. Of course not. I was just surprised to see that you weren't in bed." More like terrified.

"I'm used to going days without sleep, and if I do, it's isn't for long. I've been up for hours."
Good to know for the future.

"Why are you awake?" She says with suspicion in her voice.

"I usually go to work about this time. I work in warehouse 1. I'm a builder."

Her face contorts into one of utter shock. What did I say?

"You make those things?"
Her voice spitting out venom with her words. Oh shit, Logan, stop fucking up.

"Well yeah, it's the only work I can get since I don't have much education. I need to support Emily the best I can. She's my responsibility. I would do anything to take care of her; she's all I have."

With that, her anger seems to subside. Years living with Em have just paid off. Thanks sis.

"Sorry, I uh don't have good experiences with those things."

"Well, I was going to ask later, but now's as good a time as ever." I want to know everything about her. Where she's from, where she goes when she wants to be alone. All of it.

"What do you want to know?"

"Everything."

And she begins. Her mother and father committed suicide right after she was born. A regular old Romeo and Juliet scenario. (Another story from my great grandparent's generation) She grew up with her mom's sister and her husband. They couldn't have children of their own, so they were happy to adopt Paityn. She had a pretty normal childhood until she found out her adoptive parents were hunters. Their sole focus in life was to take down the Safety-Robos.

Paityn soon after joined the family business. She got so caught up into it that it almost drove her mad. Her parents made her vow that she would never hunt again. They promised they wouldn't either if it meant that Paityn would be safe. They had a pretty simple life for a while but earlier this year, her parents were taken away by the Safety-Robos, more like dragged away. She describes it so vividly.

They were having lunch, when they all heard a pounding at the door. Her parents told her to hide and to not come out until it was over. They told her they loved her and to be a good girl.

Even though they didn't know what was about to happen, they put up a hell of a fight. Paityn saw the whole thing go down from where she was hiding.

Wow, this girl is something. She went through all that and she's still here. I would have gone with them. If I had the chance, I would have gone with my parents. I would have left this world. No problem. What's the point of breathing when there isn't something worth breathing for?

"Wow." I don't know what else to say to her.

"Yea," she says solemnly.

"I'm so sorry."

"It's ok. I was very young. Well, it feels like I was. One year and I feel like I'm a whole different person."

She isn't though; it was only a couple of months ago. That's a lot for a 16 year-old to go through. I don't know what to say about it anymore.

"It's still not light out, do you want to go back to sleep. You're safe here; I won't let anything happen to you."

"That sounds great."

She smiles at me. Wow, she has an amazing smile. I would do anything to keep that smile on her face. With that, we both walk back into my bedroom and fall fast asleep. The second she lays her head on the pillow I hear her breathing grow heavier. Logan, don't even think about. She's going to have to leave soon. She cannot stay here; think of Emily's safety. Well, for now, she is here.

Paityn

Holy shit! Where am I? Oh, I'm at Logan's. I wake up in a cold sweat. I lean over and see that Logan has already gotten up and picked up his "bed." I finally get a good look at Logan's bedroom. I get up from a four-poster wicker bed. This bed would be more suited for a married couple. I explore the bedroom. I take inventory: 1 bed, 1 nightstand, 1 lamp, 1 desk, 1 chair, 1 armoire, no decorations, no pictures, and no color. Wow, so boring. On the 1 desk, there is a stack of clothes with a note:

'Paityn, here are some of Emily's clothes she was willing to part with. All yours. Pick and choose what you would like to wear today and the rest you can put in the empty drawer in the armoire.'

Wow, he really went above and beyond to make me feel welcomed. Oh look, he even found me a hairbrush and towel. How sweet.

I explore some more, and find that he has an attached bathroom.

Ooh, another note:

'Paityn,' Why is he so formal? 'You're welcome to use the shower. No hot water, but I'm sure you don't mind. I pried some feminine products from Emily. They're in the top shelf.'

I walk to the small shelving unit. The top shelf, as promised, has girly things. Shampoo and conditioner that smell of roses, deodorant, lotion, and soap that also smells of roses. How in the hell can he afford all this stuff? Most factory families have to share a bottle of shampoo and that's it.

I give in and take a shower using all the girly products. When I'm done, I smell like a giant rose. I walk back into the bedroom, checking to make sure no one is in there. I stride to the stack of clothes. I find some undergarments. Emily definitely has good taste in panties and bras.   I'm surprised we are pretty close in size. I choose a sundress with daisies on it. What is it with this chick and flowers? Cute but not very helpful if I have to run, but it is cute. Oh look at that, I have legs. There's a full size mirror in Logan's room, I walk over and see myself for the first time since I left home months ago. Wow. I look …

Logan

"You look beautiful." Wow she cleans up nice. She jumps at my statement.

"Sorry I didn't mean to startle you."

"It's all right, I really have to kick this jumpy habit. I've been alone for a while with no one to watch my back. And thank you, for the compliment. Emily has very good taste in fashion."

"Yea, but that dress wouldn't really be helpful if you had to run away from someone."

"Exactly!"

I offer Paityn some breakfast; she happily follows me into the kitchen where Emily is pouring water into cups for us. Emily, of course, stops clean in her tracks to gush about how cute Paityn looks in her old clothes. We sit down to eat. I'm pleasantly surprised that Emily and Paityn are a lot chattier this morning.

I don't remember being this happy and warm since mom and dad were here. Fuck, don't ruin it by thinking about mom and dad. They're gone. Emily and Paityn are here. Think about them. As they talk about how Paityn grew up and what is was like to live with her aunt and uncle, I cleaned up and slipped out of the room to open up the house and see what was happening around town.

I hear Emily yell my name out of the window as I'm walking down the cobblestones.

"Where are you off to, Logan!"

"Just for a walk," I respond.

"Take Paityn with you, I'm going next door to my nursing lesson."

I see Paityn's face through window, she looks so embarrassed; probably because Emily is treating her as if she was our child and not a fully grown women capable of staying at the house alone while we we're both out. God Emily, can you embarrass the girl anymore? I don't mind. I was going to ask her to join me, but she was happily chatting away with Emily and I didn't want to interrupt like I had the night before. Paityn walks out and the artificial sunlight reflects off her shiny black waves. I can tell she's embarrassed because she won't look up at me, just at the strappy shoes she must have slipped on before leaving the house. She has no makeup, no fancy clothes, not even anything done with her hair, but I still think she is the most beautiful thing I've ever laid my eyes on.

She finally reaches me and looks up at me with those black eyes, and I think, God, I'm so lucky she chose me to attack.

Chapter 4

"Respect yourself enough to say
"I deserve peace" and walk
away from people or things that
prevent you from attaining it."
~ Jerico Silvers

Logan

We walk on and I show her around. She doesn't have to worry about anyone noticing her because we don't have fancy screens that tell us the news. The town has a speaker system that comes on once a week to tell us how good we are doing in the factories and to keep up the good work. There is never any hard hitting news down here. Too much to announce I guess: murder, robbery, violence etc.

We go to the little stream that connects the town to the partial ocean we have left. It's unofficially called Miracle Bay because, considering it flows in and out of the putrid ocean full of animal carcasses, it still manages to be purified enough to be the towns only water supply. It's been a long time since animals with fins and flippers swam the waters. My mother told me once that there were five oceans so big that some of them had been undiscovered and untouched by humans. That's only a folk tale she told us as children but I can imagine it. I can imagine blue waters so clear they reflected like mirrors, and waters so deep that undiscovered animals roamed unseen to the human eye.

I tell this all to Paityn, and she doesn't laugh. Thank god. I don't want her to think I'm a nut job. She listens and pipes in with her own thoughts on the subject. She tells me that her uncle used to tell her about this giant sea monster people thought lived in the water and they even gave it a ridiculous name, Nessie, I think, or something like that.

We spent the day like that. Walking around, and talking. Never did we have an awkward moment. There were moments where we didn't talk, they didn't last long, but when they happened they felt comfortable.

Paityn

So this is what it feels like to be home. Don't get used to it, Paityn. Logan has been showing me around and even introducing me to all his friends and coworkers. It's a quaint little town. No one seems to recognize me. When I left the house this morning, I was a little hesitant since I've been in hiding for months. Wow, I should have done this ages ago. Logan has been getting a kick out of the stories my uncle used to tell me. He almost died laughing when I told him the one about Nessie, and I joined him. I haven't laughed that hard since my second parents went away.

Dammit Paityn, don't ruin your mood by thinking about them. You're here, with Logan, everything is ok. Once the thing in the sky that could but can't really be called the sun begins to set, we walk back to the house. I get an eerie sense as we walk up.

"Logan wait."
I stop in my tracks and listen. Logan is looking at me confused and I tell him to shut up for a second.

"It's them."

"Who?" He asks like the civilian he is.

"The Robos. I can sense them from a mile away. They're closing in. We have to get inside. They have my picture programmed into their motherboard; they're required to take me in if they see me."

"How do you know that?" Another stupid question.

"I know. Because I put it there."

He can't possibly understand.

I'm intelligent enough to hide from a bucket of bolts. The only reason I programmed my picture in their motherboards is so if I needed to get back to the nest, it would be the quickest way. I can trick them into believing that the sedative they inject me with works, but after all this time, I just became immune to it. It's rare to find someone immune to it like me. Even my aunt and uncle couldn't do that and they had been hunters most of their lives.

Logan tries to convince me no one in this town would ever do something as stupid as to try to kill or cut themselves. HA! Darling, people are so very broken, but no one seems to notice or care for that matter. I tell him wanting to die is a serious thing. It's not a way to seek attention, not that you'd want any; it's a cry for help.

Once the thought is in your head, it's all consuming. It's there every waking moment of every day. Even when you're not thinking about it, the thought doesn't linger too far away. They don't want to fight on, anymore. I know because I've felt it before.

I was tired and weak; I was done. I didn't want to talk or walk or eat or breathe. I slept because it was the only time I didn't feel pain. I hurt so badly. It was like a bottle of soda that kept being shaken, and all that was left to do was explode from all the pressure. I didn't want to be here anymore, I wanted to die. I wanted to leave everything behind. I wanted to be forgotten, and I didn't want to cause anymore anguish.

He looks at me like a lost puppy with a broken leg. I can't bare to even look at him. I can tell I hurt him in some way. And in that second, I see that all the house windows are open. Emily is home and I remember her secret. I run towards the house, leaving Logan far behind. I knew this dress would not help if I needed to run.

I barge into the house yelling for Emily. I rush from the kitchen to Emily's room. She's not here. I yell for her once more and I hear her call my name. I see her walk out of Logan's room with a boy attached to her hip. She looks at me confused. And I don't even care that she has a boy with her, I wrap my arms around her and squeeze her. I refuse to let myself cry for her safety. I know that there are probably now two guys watching me hug Emily to death.

"What was that for? Are you ok? Are you hurt?" She touches my arms, face, and stomach looking for injuries. I chuckle at her.

"I'm fine. I just … couldn't find you and I got worried."

I hesitated and Emily is questioning the validity of my answer, which I know was a lie. I can't tell her the real reason I was so worried is that I know her secret; I know that she cuts herself and I had felt a Safety-Robo near. I couldn't tell her that I thought it was coming after her, or worse, had already gotten to her before I could. I would have never forgiven myself if something happened to her.

Logan

What just happened? Paityn ran away from me so fast. I thought maybe she was upset that I looked at her with so much pity. It wasn't pity; it was guilt. Here I was, wanting to fake suicide just to see the stupid Robos, when she really wanted to do it. I could hear the pain resonate in her voice. Not once did it waver but I just felt the pain as if it was radiating off of her. How could someone with so much light in her be hiding so much darkness?

I didn't realize she didn't run away from me specifically until I heard her screaming for Emily. At that instant, I felt as though she knew something I didn't, and I ran as fast as I could into the house. I came in right when Paityn found Emily with a look of utter shock plastered onto her beautiful profile. I didn't know what shocked her more, finding her or finding her with a random guy attached to her hip. Wait what? Who's that guy?

Play it cool Logan.

"Hey Em, who's your friend?"

I try to act cool and not like I'm not about to detach him from my little sister's hip using much force. She finally notices that I'm in the room and practically jumps away from the guy.

"Oh Logan, this is James. You said that we could have him over for dinner, and he was in the neighborhood so I invited him. I hope you don't mind."

She's fidgeting. She never does that. She's usually so graceful and now she's a nervous wreck. Be nice Logan. Put on a show.

"Nice to meet you, I've heard so much about you."

"Likewise. Sorry about the intrusion, Emily told me she already gotten the ok from you."

He looks at her, I know he's teasing her but she blushes guiltily. It's kind of funny to see Emily so flustered. She must really like this James guy to go through all this trouble just to get him to come to dinner. Okay he can stay.

"It's all right. I was about to start dinner anyway. You guys can sit in the living area; I need to speak to Paityn in my room for a second."

Try to keep your composure, Logan.

I grab Paityn by her elbow, and walk to my room. She's hiding something from me, and that's not ok. I let her into my life and my home. When it comes to Emily, she HAS to tell me everything.

When we get to my room, I pace around, trying to cool off. What the hell, Paityn, you can't fucking scare me like that.

"What the hell, Paityn, you can't fucking scare me like that!"

She's looking down at her feet and doesn't respond. I look at her, and she looks torn. Like she wants to say something but is too scared to do so.

"Well!"

She jumps. Logan chill. Don't scare the girl.

"I was scared, ok? I felt the Robos coming and I just thought ..."

I cut her off.

"You thought what? That Emily tried to kill herself and they came for her?"

"No, I did think they came for her but not because she tried to kill herself. Because she's the one they're looking for."

What? What does she mean? Why would they be looking for Emily!

Paityn

I sit down and take a deep breathe. I don't want to out Emily. I like her a lot. As long as I'm here, she's in great danger. But as long as I'm here, I'm going to protect her. I will not let anything or anyone touch her. She's the closest thing I have to a family anymore and I will protect my family better than the last time. I tell him everything. I start at the beginning.

After my parents got dragged away, a fire was lit deep down. And for weeks I let that fire grow from little embers. It intensified into a raging fire in my soul. I know I had promised that I wasn't going to hunt anymore, but I couldn't just sit around the rest of my life doing nothing. I had to do something. So I went into the kitchen grabbed a knife, sharpened it, and slashed my wrists. And I didn't stop, not until the Robo smashed through the door. I blacked out, not from the sedative but from the blood loss. I would never let myself actually black out in a normal hunting situation, but it wasn't a normal hunting situation. I was out for blood.

I woke up in the nest. The nest is where they keep all the people they take away. The nest is divided into different sectors: one for eating disorders, cutting, and suicide. I was in the suicide sector since I slashed my wrists so much. I'd recognize it anywhere, the clinical smell of everything; the bright white walls and everything so comfortably predictable. I knew this place like the back of my hand; ironically, it was my second home. I felt a pang of pain when I realized that they weren't here with me, or in the building anymore. They were probably long gone by now.

Logan stops me. "Wait. What do they do with the people? Why would they keep them in a building? I thought they healed you and brought you back."

I gawk at him. For a smart guy, he really has no clue. It's going to crush him, but he needs to know.

There's a knock at the door and we both jump. "Come in." Logan says surprisingly calm.

Emily walks in and asks what we were doing in the bedroom for so long. I jump in then.

"I wasn't feeling so well so I was lying down, and Logan was watching over me. Right Logan?"

I plead at him with my eyes. Don't tell her. Please. Not yet?

"Right. But she's okay now so we'll be out in a second. Ok, sis?"

She looks weary, but believes it. She gives us five minutes and she walks out of the room.

"We're not done. I like you Paityn, but I don't know you. I brought you here, and you've been great; but this is Emily we're talking about. She's all I got. And I have to protect her."

That set me off. What do you think I was doing? Today was perfect and he got to know me. Apparently not well enough.

"That's what I was trying to do! I ran in here and went into every room looking for Emily. You have no idea how scared I was. I've been alone for so long, and then you show up. I didn't have to worry about losing anyone. Now there's you and Emily. I care about you both so much and I would do anything to make sure you're safe."

With that, he stalks out of the room, leaving me alone with my thoughts. How did I screw this up already? I was doing so well. Logan's never going to understand. Maybe I should leave well enough alone. Logan and Emily don't need any more complications in their life. If I leave, they'll be better off.

Logan

Who does she think she is? I can protect Emily on my own. I go into the kitchen and Emily knows something is off. I tell her everything is fine but she won't believe me.

"You're keeping something from me."
She puts her hands on her hips; she's not going to let this one go.

"We have a guest, Emily, it would be rude to speak about our personal problems in front of him."

I know I put James in an awkward position but it was the only way she was going to drop it.

"Fine. You took so long, I made dinner. Hope you don't mind. Where is Paityn? The food is going to get cold."

"She's in my room. I'll go get her."

I shouldn't have been so hard on her. Why did I mess this up? She was just worried about Emily. I need to apologize.

I walk into my room. Paityn isn't anywhere to be seen. I look in my bathroom, nothing. I walk out of my room calmly. I don't want Emily to worry.

Where the hell is she? I go into Emily's room, check the living room, then go outside to Emily's garden but Paityn is gone. Oh no. I made her leave. I shouldn't have yelled at her. What if a Robo got her? I would never forgive myself if something happens to her.

I walk into the kitchen. James can't know. Emily is going to beat it out of me if she has to, so I have to get James to leave.

"James?"

"Yea?" He responds quickly.

"I'm so sorry but something has come up, I need to be alone with my sister."

Emily looks mortified. She goes on a rampage about how rude I am being to her guest, when she's been nothing but nice to Paityn.

"So you were just being nice to Paityn because she's our guest?"

Now I have her. I need to make this fast, Paityn could be long gone by now. I need to get her back. She needs to know how sorry I am. I can't lose her just yet.

"Of course not! But James is my guest and he's waited long enough to eat dinner, so go get Paityn and we can talk later."

With her hand on her hips and her stern look, she looks just like mom. I can't say no to her. James stands and places his arm on Emily's shoulder. Maybe he understands and he'll leave. Please leave.

"The lady has spoken, I'm not going anywhere, Logan."

Excuse me? Who the hell does he think he is? He better get his stinkin' paws off my sister before I rip them off.

Emily intervenes just as I was about to rip his head off.

"You can't talk to him like that! You are my guest, but he is my brother. There has been too much fighting tonight. James, I think you should leave!"

"I'm not going anywhere."

His smile contorts into one of pure evil. Oh, fuck no. He's dead.

Paityn

I can't believe I did that. I should have fought harder to stay. NO. They don't need someone like me messing up their lives.

I keep walking. To where, I'm not sure. I end up at Miracle Bay; I just need time to think. I need time to plan what I'm going to do next. I could go back. Maybe Logan cooled off by now. Maybe he'll forgive me and let me stay.

Then what, Paityn? Are you going to marry him and live happily ever after? That doesn't happen to people like me.

What if I don't go back and something happens? I can still feel the Robos in the area, but at the moment, I just don't care. They are not my top priority.

I walk back to the house. Slowly and cautiously I approach the house and immediately sense something is wrong.

Oh no. I run up the steps, and press my ear to the door. I can't hear anything so I slowly open the door. I creep along the wall and head towards the kitchen.

Everything is in shambles. Fuck! What happened! I stop and listen, nothing. I hear something; I hear an almost inaudible groan coming from the kitchen. I walk in slowly, making sure no Robos or anything else that can harm me is in there. I walk closer to where the moans and groans are coming from. I see him … Oh no. No. No. No. This isn't right.

"Logan!!!"

Everything becomes extremely slow. I fall to my knees next to him. I did this! Please! NO. NO. NO.

I put my head in my hands and draw my knees up close. I want to cry. I want to be invisible and make it all go away. I haven't felt this since my parents went away, I don't think I've ever cried.

I hear Logan stir.

"Paityn?"

He's barely audible. Oh thank god! I touch him, everywhere. Making sure nothing is broken or bruised but mainly because I want to make sure he's actually here breathing; that I'm not just dreaming. He tries to get up and I hug him, not caring that we have never been this close.

Wait. Logan's here. Where is … CRAP!

"Logan ... where's Emily?" Stay calm. Don't scare him.

"SHIT!!"

He gets up in record time. He bolts from one room to another. Too late, I guess.

Logan comes back and runs his fingers through his hair. I want to do that. I pout. PAITYN, this is not the time, now focus.

Logan is pacing and mumbling about James being a bastard. He's usually so composed and calm. I hate seeing him like this. I need to fix this. He took care of me, now I need to take care of him. I walk up to him and place my hand on his shoulder; he winces. Ouch. I like touching you. God, Paityn, stop it!

"I'm sorry. I'm going to get her back I promise, but you need to tell me what happened." Ok. Good.

He looks conflicted. I see anger and fire in his eyes, and then it subsides to something sweet but carnal.

He grabs both of my shoulders, holds me at arm's length and looks at me. I mean really looks at me with those smoldering green eyes. I squirm. Wow. I melt. Then all of a sudden, he's in my arms. His arms wrapped around my waist, head against my chest. I feel him convulsing as his sobs escape his mouth. Oh Logan. We sit on the floor, amongst the rubble. I stroke his beautiful dark brown hair. It's so soft.

I wish we could stay like this forever, but we have pressing matters.

"Logan?"

I lift him off my chest and look at him. He looks so broken. This boy I met only a few days ago has become a broken man, where as he used to be strong and confident. I broke him.

I choke back tears because this is not the time. I need him to get up and tell me what happened, and then I will finish explaining why Emily was taken. He's so not going to like this.

"He took her. Paityn, he took Emily! I couldn't do anything. This is all my fault. If I hadn't been upset with you, we both could have fought him. I did this."

WHAT?!?!

Chapter 5

"The way I see it, every life is a pile of good things and bad things. The good things don't always soften the bad things but vice versa, the bad things don't necessarily spoil the good things or make them unimportant."

~The 11th Doctor

Logan

She looks at me as if I just said something incredibly stupid. Ouch. My head hurts.

"How could you think this is your fault? I was the one that left. If I wasn't so selfish and thinking of myself, I could have saved Emily. Logan, I'm so sorry."

We stare at each other, both understanding that we shouldn't worry about whose fault it was. We need to think of a plan to get my sister back. We get up together, mostly with her help since I'm so weak. Damn James, what was that thing he shocked me with? I've never seen anything like it. I can't believe I was so stupid! SO STUPID! God Emily, I hope you're okay.

Paityn helps me walk over to the couch, which is way more comfortable than the floor. Paityn walks away and into the kitchen. Don't leave again. Please. She walks back in with a glass of water and insists I drink all of it.

"So what happened? Tell me everything. Start from the beginning."

Wow, so calm. How can you be so calm? Maybe it's for my sake. I start from when I figured out she had left. I told her that I told James he needed to leave and that's when everything went to hell.

Robos busted through the kitchen door and grabbed Emily. James kicked me in the back of the legs, forcing me to my knees. He had that thing in his hand while he kept me on my knees. He shocked me in the back of the neck. I watched everything happen, and I couldn't do anything to help her. I can still hear her high-pitched screaming in my ears. She's small and dainty but she put up a hell of a fight. I saw her thrashing, and even got away at one point.

But then one of the Robos injected her with some bright red liquid and she collapsed in its arms. That's when James put his shocking weapon to my temple and I was out like a light.

I finally got to see the Robos. Be careful what you wish for I guess.

She stares at me with those eyes. God, I can look into those for the rest of my life. Logan! Now is not the time. She looks down at her hands and puts her head into them.

"What?"

"I have to tell you something, and you are so not going to like it."

What?

She takes a deep breath and starts her story.

Paityn has been a hunter her whole life. Her whole family was hunters, that's how her real parents died. What she had said before wasn't a lie, they did kill themselves for the sake of love but they were on a hunt, and it didn't go as planned. The Robos got into their heads and finished them off.

"What do you mean they finished them off? Do you mean they killed them? Is that why they never come back?"

"Robos cannot kill people. It's against their programming. The rooms they put people in are like holographic prison cells."

She goes on telling me about these cells. They show people exactly what they're thinking when they try to kill themselves. That the people they love will be better off without them, that they'll feel better where they'll end up, that all the pain goes away. The Robos are trying to break the people. They can't kill people but they break them so they kill themselves.

What?!?

"Wait. They drag people out of their homes as they TRY to kill themselves just to put them in a room so they CAN kill themselves. That makes no sense."

"Don't you see? A dead empty body isn't of use to them. They need a body with a soul, a soul they can take."

No way! I don't believe it.

Paityn

He looks like I just dropped a bomb. I can't tell him. This is going to destroy him.

"Logan I'm so sorry."

"Why?"

This is it. He won't be able to look at me after this.

"Logan, the hierarchy is committing genocide. They make people's lives as desolate as possible so they want to kill themselves. When they try, the Robos drag them to the nest; break them so they do kill themselves so they can take their souls. They are doing this to rid the world of humans. They don't want the world infested with us poor, unfortunate souls.

The Robos are a vital part of their society, like servants. They are making an army, hence, you being a builder. Once they clean this area out, they will move on to the next and the next. You build Robos to take your souls and you ship out Robos to take other people's souls."

"What! You have got to be kidding me!"

He gets up and walks over to the closet grabs his coat and puts it on. Where is he going?

"Where are you going?"

"Thanks for the insight but what has all this got to do with finding my sister!"

Fuck he's pissed.

I get up and try to remain calm. He needs to understand.

"Logan, haven't you noticed how Emily likes her privacy? She is a little too happy, almost like she's faking it?"

"Paityn, you need to fucking spit it out or I'm going to walk out that door and look for my sister without you!"

Now I'm mad. Logan, listen to me please.

"The whole fucking world has tracking chips in them! They make parents "vaccinate" their kids when they're born. Robos know where you are and what you're thinking at all times. They know every move you're making. The second the thought of hurting yourself pops up in that little insignificant brain of yours, they find you.

BUT I've heard of someone who got away. A family who hid their kid from the vaccination, how I don't know, but they did. The hierarchy got whiff of this and they don't like it. These people figured out how to kill the chip out of their kid and the recipe is out there somewhere, in someone."

"I don't get it."

Really do I have to spell it out for you?

"Logan! It's EMILY! Are you that dense? You're sister is living with the formula inside her. She is the formula! Your parents died fighting to keep that formula from the Robos and the hierarchy. Don't you get it?"

He stops and just stares at me. Now I've done it. I broke him. I think I can actually hear his heart shattering.

"No. No. No. NO!"

Fuck.

"Logan, calm down."

He walks toward me. He has a crazy look in his eyes. I'm a goner. This is it. This is how I die.

"Don't you fucking tell me to calm down."

He whispers. Walking towards me, he backs me into a corner.

"So you're telling me my parents were hunters and that they put something inside my sister that can

81

save the world. But the hierarchy wants to kill her because of it?"

"Logan …"

He explodes with rage. He punches the wall right next to my face, catching me off guard.

"Don't you Logan me!"

Fuck. He's scary.

"Did you know all this time? Is that why you attacked me that day? Has all this been a lie?"

"Of course not! I had no idea until I met Emily. I promise! The night you brought Emily candy, she hugged you and her shirt lifted up. I saw her scars, Logan. I thought she was just a myth, but I knew it was her. I should have told you right there and then, but you wouldn't have believed me. You have to understand, I wasn't sure and now I'm too late. I am so sorry."

I reach out for him and he retreats but gives in. I rest my palm on his cheek and he leans into it.

"I. Am. So. Sorry. I promise I'll get her back. I will; even if it's the last thing I do."

"Ok. Ok. Where do we start?"

Now this is my department. This I can do.

Logan

I can't do this. Emily is the formula? I can't wrap my head around all this information. My parents weren't hunters. I remember; everything was normal. We had a NORMAL childhood. No tests, no formulas.

Paityn is rummaging in our attic, looking for anything that would give us information about my family, or the formula. I can't face it all so I'm in Emily's room. Everything is in its place, just how Emily liked it. I sit on her bed, looking at it all from her point of view. Did she really hurt herself? What did she have to be sad about? I know she took our parents departure hard, but could she really do it? She was always so happy, so cheerful and so Emily. Emily has always been there for anyone who needed help. She was a great listener and always knew what to say to make people feel better. She was a great friend and a great person. How could someone like that be so sad, sad enough to open her own flesh? I don't believe it. I can't, she wouldn't.

I get up and head to her drawer set. I open it and see her clothes, everything folded neatly in piles. I can't help it. I rip everything out; I go from one drawer to the next. All my anger is boiling over; I can't help it. I need to find it. I need proof. How can she do this to me?!? I wanted so much for her! I rip her vanity apart, digging through her closet, laundry basket. Anything and everything I can get my hands on flies across the room.

Where the fuck is it!!!!

I pace back and forth and look around the room I just destroyed. I look at the bed, now covered with clothes I just flung out of all the drawers. I walk over to it and just stare at it. I flipped this whole room upside down, and the last thing left is the bed. I lift the mattress off of the bedpost, and knock it over. There they were, tons of them. Color coded and different sizes and shapes of blades. That's so like Emily to color code her weapons of choice.

I hear a creak in the floorboards.
There she is, always shows up when I need her.

"Find what you were looking for?"

"Not exactly."

"Hmm. It's just like her to color code her blades."

"Yea. Did you find anything?" I ask, wanting to change the subject.

"Not exactly. But I did find the blueprints of the house.

She starts walking out of the room, but she turns back and looks at me. She walks over and grabs my hand, then starts walking out with me. Do I look as broken as I feel? She walks over to the kitchen table where the remnants of Emily's dinner lay. Paityn swipes everything off the table with both her arms, leaving it empty. She lays down the blue print to the house and rolls it out.

"I've read tons of blue prints but this one looks different. The ink is all smeared and some words are missing."

"Well it must be really old, this house belonged to my grandparents and, when my mother inherited it, my dad remolded it to fit both Emily and me."

"These were your dad's plans for the remodel. What I can't understand is why it doesn't look like the finished product."

"What do you mean?"

"Look, there are 3 extra rooms in the print, a whole other level of the house. It looks like the only way to get there is through the kitchen, but I don't see an entry way on the print."

I remember. When Emily and I were really small, we were playing outside with a ball our parents had found in the dumpster and fixed up for us. We didn't have many toys so when they came about, our parents couldn't keep us in, even for lunch. I remember. Em had thrown the ball into a bush and I had to dig it out. I got a thorn in my hand and went inside to get mom to take it out before it really got dug in there. I opened the front door of the house and I heard mom and dad in the kitchen.

I wanted to scare them, so I crept along the wall so they couldn't see me from where they were standing. I heard them whispering about Em. How she was doing better with the new treatment and how she wasn't reacting badly to the serum. I peeked around the corner and saw them open the floor. I ran out to tell Emily about the floor opening and she wouldn't believe me.

Then I ran back inside with Emily, and my mom and dad were in the kitchen like nothing had happen. Mom was cooking and dad was sitting at the dinning room table with one of his books. I guess I made myself forget since it never really happened.

Paityn

He looks really distant for a while, and really quiet. What now?

He walks away towards the other end of the kitchen and starts jumping and hopping from one spot to another. He's gone crazy.

"What are you doing?"

"I remember. Well, not really, I thought I had just imagined it. When I was small, I saw my parents open the floor. If I jump around, I might be able to find where it sounds most hollow."

I can't help but smirk. He looks so silly hopping around the kitchen. He looks so serious but continues hopping, and right in the center of the kitchen, we hear the hollow sound we were listening for.

"Found it."

He drops to all fours and starts clawing at the floor. I rush over to help him; we get the floorboards to lift enough to completely pull them out. After ripping out floorboards, there is a perfectly circular opening in the ground, narrow enough to fit one person, with a ladder that leads down the hole.

"Age before beauty." I motion towards the floor.

"All right I'll go. If I die, I blame you."

"Just go, would you?"

He starts climbing down the ladder. After he goes down about 5 rungs, I can no longer see him. About 30 seconds later, he yells up for me to start heading down.

"Hold on a sec."

I run into Logan's room and rummage through his drawers in hopes of finding a flashlight of some sort. I find an old lantern in the back of Logan's closet and head to the kitchen again. It's too quiet.

"Logan!"

I yell down the hole. I hear nothing back. Fuck! This isn't good.

I clamor down the hole, as fast as I can. When I get to the bottom and see a tunnel that leads to a lightened room. I walk cautiously towards the light.

"Logan?"

"I'm in here."

He sounds so defeated. I walk in and see this giant room with all sorts of gadgets everywhere. Each wall is covered, floor to ceiling, with weapons. In the middle of the room is a table full of bottles of colored liquids that seem to glow. I can see a door that leads to another room. I leave Logan to his own devices for a moment so he can take it all in.

I open the steel door that is branded with some strange symbol that resembles a fiery red crown made of thorns. My mouth drops the instant I realize what this room is. Pristine white walls, the clinical smell; I recognize it so well. How the hell did they replicate it?!?

"What is this?"

"It's a holographic prison cell. How did your parents even do this?" I say, thinking aloud.

"So these are the things that make people commit suicide, in the end I mean."

"Yes …" I wonder if it's functional.

I storm out and look for a switch of any kind. I need to know if it works. Who the hell were his parents? How did they have the technology and resources to build this place? Who were these people? I'm touching and flipping everything, carefully of course, to see if I can find anything that will turn on the cell.

"What are you looking for?"

"The switch to turn on the room." I respond coolly.

"Are you insane? Why would you want to turn it on?"

Logan

"Ah Ha! I found it!"

She is not going in there!

"You are not going in there, Paityn!"

"Do you trust me?" she questions.

"That's beside the point."

"I need to know. Trust me."

"Fine I'm going in with you."

"The Hell you are?!? I need to go in there by myself, Logan. You need to stay out here to turn it off."

"Over my dead body!"

She's INSANE!

"Logan … you need to understand! I need you out here. Someone needs to turn this thing off. I've been in one of these things; I can handle it. I promise."

"You've been in one! Why the hell would you let it go that far! Do you have any sense of self-preservation?"

"Of course I've been in one! I've been in the nest. It's part of what I do. You know me. You've known who I am this whole time. I can't change who I am. I can't change where I came from. And what I do is going to save your sister, if you forgot! I might not have any sense of so-called self-preservation, but I have enough sense to know where my priorities lie!"

Well that shut me up. I hate it when she's right.

"All right. Show me how to do the thing."

She explains that she can't be in there for more than 10 minutes. The room, if she's correct, is equipped with multiple weapons to off herself with. She said she's probably the best hunter she's run into, not being cocky at all, but even the cell can push her off the edge. She can't promise she'll be ok when she comes out, but she has to know.

Why does she need to know if it works? How in the hell will that help save Emily? She tells me that when she comes out I need to remind her that I'm real and that this is really happening; anything to make her settle back into her normal persona.

"All right I got it. Go. Before I change my mind."

"Ok. Remember. No more than 10 minutes, Logan. It's really important!"

She starts walking towards the steel door and hesitates for a moment. She turns to face me, then runs towards me. She wraps her arms around my neck and firmly plants a kiss on my lips. I kiss her back. It was one of those kisses that makes you feel exactly what you were hoping the other person felt. I squeezed her back and refused to break our kiss.

It was the kind of kisses to end all kisses. The last kiss, the one that made me feel like she was saying goodbye. I won't let you go that easy, Paityn. Not now, not ever.

"Don't you dare say goodbye."

"Never."

With that she walks into the room and I follow behind her to lock it. I walk to the switch and flip it on.

I hear her scream in agony, and run towards the steel door. I can't take this. I can't hear her be tortured for 10 minutes. I can't do this. Get a grip, Logan! Trust that she can do this. I sit cross-legged in front of the door and realize that there is a clock right besides it. 2 minutes. 8 more to go. I feel like a helpless, lost child waiting for someone to find me.

I look up at the timer and see that only a few seconds has passed. I can't help but feel that this clock is taking ages. I get up and start pacing in front of the door; back and forth, back and forth.

You can't do this to yourself, Logan. She WILL be ok. I walk around the room looking at everything my parents left behind. There are gadgets hanging on all of the walls, and I have no idea what any of them do. This is what my parents did? How could they hide all this from us?

I walk over to the other end of the room, being wary of the clock that is slowly but surely ticking down. The bright colored liquids have my attention for just a moment. Then I hear Paityn scream my name.

I run towards the door and am about to open it when I see there is still 5 minutes on the clock.

Logan, don't open it. She can handle it. Walk away. I walk back to the startling liquids that glow in the light. I circle them, in a way I feel as though I'm missing something. My brain is trying to remember something that I can't bring to the surface. My childhood that was once normal and sane has now become so hazy to me. Everything that I believed true is now a lie. My brain is fried. I look and the clock has come down to 1 minute. I run to the switch and countdown with the clock from 60. 52 ... 48 ... 33 ... 27 ... 12 ... 5 ... NOW!

I turn the switch and run to the steel door. I unlock it and swing it open. I see Paityn lying in a pool of red liquid. I rush to her and shake her.

"Paityn!! You need to wake up… Paityn!"

This is not how this is going to end. She can't die like this. It wasn't even 10 minutes. Did I do something wrong? I can't lose her. I just can't. Oh god!

Paityn

I hear someone calling to me; but that's impossible I'm dead. I'm gone. No longer existent. I couldn't be here anymore. It's my fault Emily was taken. If I had never come here, she would still be safe. Logan's life was ruined because of me. He doesn't need me to get Emily back; he can figure it out. He figured me out, something my parents couldn't even do. He's so amazing and deserves someone just as amazing as him. I could never be what he needs. He needs someone whole; I'm too broken.

I was shattered into a million pieces a long time ago. I lost pieces, gave away some, and some just fell off, as time went on. Now I'm empty, no pieces to worry about. I can feel nothing. I am nothing.

Epilog

"Above all, I just want you to know how significant you are in case no other human in this cruel world tells you so. You do not have to be a symphony or a masterpiece to do good in this world.

There is so much love to give and receive if only you allow your heart to be open. Stretch it out as wide as the horizon, fill your soul with all the world's beauty as the tragic things in your eyes crash down around you like ash.

Let nothing stop you. Not one damn thing.

So, I guess all that is left, that which was left in the beginning, is to love every single thing that surrounds you, as if death was soon to come for is all."

~Christopher Poindexter

www.ingramcontent.com/pod-product-compliance
Lightning Source LLC
Chambersburg PA
CBHW070345130626
46556CB00007B/3042